This book belongs to:

Diona Kay

_G-ma 9/05_

Written by Kath Smith
Illustrated by Caroline Jayne Church
Designed by Andrea Newton
Language consultant: Betty Root

This is a Parragon Publishing book
First published in 2002

Parragon Publishing
Queen Street House
4 Queen Street
Bath BA1 1HE, UK

ISBN 1-84273-423-7

The Little Friends
Fairies are Fun

I love You!

p

Silly Fairy Lily

Lily was a fairy who
Was always lots of fun.
But sometimes Lily's jokes went wrong
And upset everyone.

She wasn't really naughty,
But she didn't take much care.
In her trail, she always left
Disaster everywhere.

She borrowed Heather's magic book,
And let the spells escape.
She stirred her drink with Daisy's wand,
Until it lost its shape.

She upset Princess Sarah
And really made her frown.
Poor Sarah was a leprechaun,
Complete with dress and crown.

Sir Dave was most annoyed one day.
"She made my best horse shrink!
What a silly girl!" he cried.
"If only she would think!"

One day Fairy Lily met
The nephew of Sir Dave,
And saw the trouble that is caused
By those who misbehave!

He used her wand for fighting,
And spilled her fairy dust.
Then raced around while Lily cried,
"Oh, do please stop! You must!"

As he smashed some glasses
(She heard the awful clink),
Lily yelled in horror,
"If only you would think!"

As soon as she had spoken,
She laughed aloud in glee.
"I've heard those words before,"
She said, "but they were said to me!"

"I guess I should be grateful
To you, you little tyke,
For showing me so clearly
Just what my ways are like."

Now Lily is more careful,
And looks at all the facts.
Before she does a silly thing,
She thinks before she acts!

Clever Fairy Heather

Heather was the smartest
Of the fairies in the land.
So people always came to her—
She loved to lend a hand.

No matter WHAT the problem was,
WHATEVER it involved,
As soon as Heather tackled it,
You knew it would be solved.

"Don't you worry!" she would smile,
As helpful as can be.
"I will find an answer.
Just you wait and see!"

Now Heather had her problems, too,
Which she really longed to share.
But no one took the time to listen—
They did not seem to care.

When Heather tried to tell her friends
About her little troubles,
All they seemed to want to do
Was speak of their own muddles.

Though Heather was a patient girl,
She finally slammed her door,
And shouted in her loudest voice,
"I won't listen anymore!"

The other fairies were amazed.
"Has Heather gone on strike?
It really isn't like her ...
it's just not Heather-like!"

Then Daisy saw just what was wrong,
"Oh, now I understand!
When Heather has a problem,
Who gives a helping hand?"

Lily blushed a shade of pink.
"I really must agree.
Because I don't say thank you
Whenever she helps me.

19

"It's time that we said thank you
For all her good advice,
And showed her just how much we care
By doing something nice."

So Lily gave her bluebells,
And polished Heather's wings.
While lazy Daisy cleaned her house
And fixed some broken things.

"I might be smart," Heather said,
And hugged them happily.
"But not enough to realize
What friends you are to me!"

21

Lazy Fairy
Daisy

Daisy was a fairy who
Was lazy as can be.
Whenever someone asked for help,
She'd yawn and say, "Why me?"

When other fairies teased her,
And called her lazybones,
She'd mutter, "Words can't hurt me.
They're not like sticks and stones."

Why she was so idle
Was very hard to say.
(The only reason was, I fear,
That she was born that way!)

So while the others rushed around
Preparing for the ball,
Daisy lounged around and yawned,
"What's the matter with you all?"

She watched them cut their costumes out,
Then neatly sew each dress.
But Daisy didn't lend a hand—
She just could not care less!

Even Princess Lucy,
Who liked to dream a lot,
Had made herself a costume,
But Daisy just would not!

The night before the summer ball
Poor Daisy saw her fate.
"I haven't got a costume,
And now it is too late!"

"Don't worry," whispered Lucy,
Who had a bright idea.
"You will have a dress to wear.
Now wipe away that tear."

Soon Daisy's friends were busy.
They stitched throughout the night,
Until they'd made a costume
That fitted her just right.

"Oh, thank you!" exclaimed Daisy,
Smiling now with pleasure.
"Today I've learned a lesson—
And one I'll always treasure!

"For when there is a job to do
Now I understand.
The work is done in half the time,
If we all lend a hand!

"I won't be lazy anymore—
Not when there's work to do!
So when this ball is over,
I'll straighten up for you!"